Green Angel

Green Angel

SCHOLASTIC INC.

New York Toronto London Auckland Sydney
Mexico City New Delhi Hong Kong Buenos Aires

ALICE HOFFMAN

ISBN 0-439-44385-7   12 11   6 7 8/0

Printed in the U.S.A. 01   First Scholastic paperback printing, October 2003

The text type was set in Adobe Garamond.

Book design by Elizabeth B. Parisi

Green Angel

Heart

This is how it happened

I once believed that life was a gift. I thought whatever I wanted I would someday possess. Is that greed, or only youth? Is it hope or stupidity? As far as I was concerned the future was a book I could write to suit myself, chapter after chapter of good fortune. All was right with the world, and my place in it was assured, or so I thought then. I had no idea that all stories unfold like white flowers, petal by petal, each in its own time and season, dependent on circumstance and fate. The future is something no one can foretell.

My family had always lived on the ridgetop above the village in a county where days were sunny and warm. At twilight, dusk wove across the meadows like a dream of the next day to come. People said we were blessed, and maybe that was true. My father was honest and strong. My mother collected blue jay feathers, preferring them to her pearls. My little sister, Aurora, was as wild as she was beautiful. Aurora could climb a tree in the blink of an eye. She could disappear into the woods like moonlight. She could dance for hours and never tire.

I was the least among them, nothing special, just a girl. I was a moody, dark weed; still, they called me Green because of my talents in the garden. My mother was the one who taught me everything I knew — to bury old boots beneath peach trees to ensure they'll bear the sweetest fruit, to douse roses with vinegar-water to chase away beetles, to plant when the moon wanes and harvest when it is on the rise.

My sister, Aurora, could never sit still and pay attention. She chased after frogs, she trailed her prettiest dresses through the mud, she stole apples from our neighbor's orchard, she laughed so hard whenever her snappy little terrier, Onion, danced on his hind legs, we thought she'd never come to her senses. Aurora didn't listen to a word my mother said. We all knew she couldn't stay in one place any longer than moonlight could. Every time she ran through the garden the warblers and sparrows would follow her. Bees would drink the sweat from her skin and never once sting. My mother laughed and said the honey in our hives would taste especially wild and sweet.

At night, Aurora and I shared a room. Aurora slept without blankets or pillows, her pale hair streaming. Once or twice I had awoken to spy her curled up on the floor with her little dog. As she dreamed, white moths hovered above her, more drawn to her than they were to the moon or to the lantern my father kept on the porch, a beacon that signaled to anyone who might lose his way in the woods.

Aurora was made out of laughter and moonlight, but I was nothing like that. Unlike my fearless sister, I was afraid of blackbirds and thunder. I couldn't get a good night's sleep unless I had three feather pillows under my head and two down quilts covering me. But I was the one who could sit in the garden for hours, unmoving, as I watched seedlings unfold. I was Green, with my long, dark hair and my endless patience. A weed who grew too tall. I was Green, who never smiled at anyone, who preferred roses and asparagus to people. I was shy and ill at ease, uncomfortable with girls my own age, unwilling to talk to the boys at school. I wasn't good company, that was true, and people avoided me, but that was all right. I was too busy dreaming.

My head was in the clouds even on the days we went into town. I didn't notice when people said hello to me. I was too busy thinking about the future to come. When my mother sent us to do her shopping, I was too timid to enter the market and sent my sister in my place.

Aurora laughed at how fainthearted I was.

They won't bite you, she said.

All the same, I kept my distance. I didn't mind if the storekeepers favored my sister. They gave her sweets, mints and sugared almonds, which she would share evenly, fifty-fifty. Aurora always remembered me. I was a reflection of what she was, a dark pond to mirror her moonlight. I hugged her, grateful that she didn't notice I was less than she was. I ran home with her through the woods even though she was faster and more graceful than I would ever be. I didn't care who preferred my good-natured sister. I was Green, who was more comfortable in shadows. Green, who faded in the light of my sister. How could I not defer to her? The moon itself paled compared to her. Even the white moths would rather circle around her than fly into the sky up above.

But I knew how to listen. I was the one who paid attention to the lessons my mother taught us.

I learned that the roots of the foxglove were poisonous, that verbena could quiet headaches, that quince could be boiled into a sticky, delicious jam. In time, I knew more than my mother. Soon, she began to turn to me for advice. When should we harvest? When should we sow? What would do best in the patch of sunlight beside the gate?

I could whisper to the old, twisted wisteria and it would turn green at my urging. I could encourage the sweet peas to blossom with one word. Let Aurora smile at the shopkeepers and wave to the boys in the school yard. My dreams were of night-blooming flowers, white on the outside, but green as my heart on the inside, green as my garden grew.

I never complained when people didn't notice me. I was certain my time would come soon enough. There was dirt under my fingernails and I was too shy to speak, but on my next birthday I would turn sixteen. Everything would change then. I would cast away my fears and step into my future. I would comb the tangles from my hair and wash the dirt away. When I walked through town, people would whisper, *Is that Green?* And I would say, *Yes it's me, I've been here all along, but you've been too blind to see.*

I would have gone with my family on the day that it happened, but someone had to stay home and pull weeds. Someone had to coax the tomatoes into turning red and persuade the squash blossoms to bloom, and that person was me. We lived within sight of the city, which glowed silver at night and shone like gold in the afternoon. Every week we brought our vegetables across the river to sell to city people who couldn't get enough of our peas and lettuce and beans. Every week we crossed the bridge, and as we did I held my breath. I could feel happiness then.

I lived for those trips to the city. On the weeks I couldn't go, I pouted for hours. The city was my treasure, and I loved everything about it: the shops on the avenues, the books in the stalls, the chocolates weighed and measured by vendors in the streets. No one in the city cared if your hair was long and tangled, or if there was dirt under your fingernails. No one cared if you whispered a greeting to the linden trees that circled the park where we set up our stand. You could be who you wanted to be in the city. You could be whoever you were deep inside. It was like a garden of people, the only place where I didn't feel alone in a crowd.

Naturally, I wanted to go that day. It was my turn. But Aurora was still too young to stay by herself. And on this trip my father was needed to carry the heavy crates, wooden boxes overflowing from the best harvest we'd had in years. As for my mother, she was the one who drew the customers, like the white moths who were entranced by Aurora. People on the street couldn't resist my mother's sweet voice, her gentle hands, her long, black hair, raven-colored, like mine. It was clear she couldn't stay.

It made sense for me to work in the garden, for me to be the one who stayed home, but I was angry all the same. When my family set out to leave, they called good-bye, but I didn't answer. My father whistled a tune, and although the sparrows returned his call I did not. I wouldn't even look at him, even though he was so strong and so kind. I didn't say a word.

I'll bring you something special, Aurora promised. I knew she'd spend all her free time searching for a gift that would please me, a book or a bag of sweets, but I didn't blow her a kiss or wish her well.

There will be plenty of times for you to be the one to go, my mother told me. My mother, who was so beautiful, who knew the secrets of the growing season, who always assured me that everyone had her own path, and that mine could be found in the garden.

Green, my mother said to me that day, moments before they left for the city, *we're leaving you behind because you're the one who's needed most of all.*

Now that she was standing next to me, I was surprised to find that I was almost as tall as my mother. I felt my love for her in the back of my throat, like a stone, heavy, making it impossible for me to speak. I was almost a woman myself. Too old to admit I was wrong, or so I thought then. Too old to race after my mother when she turned to leave. I had too much pride to say good-bye. I kept my nose in the air and my back to them. I was Green, moody and prideful and angry.

I will forever remember that I turned away.

We had so many birds in the trees back then, and each one sang to me while I did my work. I weeded for hours, until my hands ached. Three blue jay feathers drifted down to me. I kept them in my pocket as a gift for my mother, if I decided to forgive her.

The day was perfect, cloudless and blue; still I continued to feel sorry for myself. At noon, I decided to take my lunch up to the hillside that overlooked the city. I let my sister's dog, Onion, trail after me even though he was an annoying beggar who sometimes growled when he saw me. Today Onion tolerated me because my sister wasn't there, but I knew I was just a substitute for Aurora.

It was so warm that I was tired by the time I reached the top of the hill. I can remember the way it felt to breathe in the hot, still air. The stitch in my side. The river in the distance, flat as a mirror. The brambles that had caught in my long, black hair. The blue jays' feathers in my pocket. The chattering of a wood thrush overhead. The dog whining softly. The pulse in my throat at the last moment of the world as it was.

People who were close by said they could see people jumping from the buildings, like silver birds, like bright diamonds. The ground shook, people said, but from where I stood all I could see was smoke. I could hear the whoosh of the fire all these miles away, across the river, past the woods. I could hear it as if it were happening inside my own head.

I ran down the hill so fast, my clothes were torn to shreds on the brambles. My heart was in my mouth. I thought of my mother, measuring out green beans on a scale with her gentle hands. I thought of my father, who could whistle so many tunes with such sweetness, every variety of bird in our garden would answer. I thought of my sister, whose hair was white as snow, the wild girl who never stopped to listen, always the opposite of me. My sister, who was as familiar as the moon up above, changeable, yes, but always there for me to depend upon.

Ashes had swept across the river in black whirlwinds. I ran to escape them, through the yard, into the house. But there was no escape. Embers flew in through the open windows and set the ends of my hair on fire. I wrapped a wet towel around my head. Steam rose in billows from beneath the towel and I smelled like smoke. But worst of all, the embers had flown into my eyes. My eyes burned so badly, I grew dizzy with the pain.

My sister's little dog had followed me home. He knew something was wrong and now he barked at the sky, the world, the open door, which

I ran to slam shut as I tried to stop the flow of embers. I fastened the bolt, then held my hands over my ears. I didn't want to hear the roar of the fire, so far away, across the river. I wanted silence, peace, blue skies, yesterday. But no matter what, I could hear it still. No matter what, it was burning.

I crawled under the dining room table, smelling like smoke and half-blinded by cinders. Little bits of hot embers flew under the door. Onion followed and lay shivering in my lap. I was Green, who was too shy to speak. Green, too angry to say good-bye. Green, who was always waiting for the future, biding her time. Now the future was here and the silver city across the river was on fire and I was hiding under the table, where I stayed until darkness fell.

After a while I couldn't hear the fire anymore. The dog whimpered, but I hushed him. I could barely see, but my ears were good. I was the one who could hear the wisteria unfolding. I could hear the sweet peas climbing the fence, the asparagus rising through the soil. Now, I was listening harder than ever. I was waiting for my family to come home. All they had to do was run from the fire. All they needed was to cross the river. Swim, if they must. Crawl, if need be. Find their way home in the dark, in the whirlwinds, in the burning embers. Surely they would appear if only I waited long enough. I was patient Green, after all. Green, who knew how to listen.

They were in the city for only a single day. Luck couldn't be as bad as that, could it? Was that the way the future worked? Unknowable, unchangeable, always uncertain. They might have gone to the city the day before or the day after. They might have been stopped by the rising of the drawbridge, by a bee sting, by a sudden storm. They might have not gone at all.

But they were there when it happened. And I was not.

It was days before I stopped listening for them, my mother's footsteps, my father's whistle, my sister's wild laughter. I had already decided that I would not allow myself to cry until they came home safely. Tears now would be an admission that they were gone. That I could stop listening. I wasn't ready for that.

Every morning I rose from my fitful sleep in the bed I'd made beneath the table expecting to find a trail of my family's footsteps on our dusty floor. I would embrace them and tell them how much I loved them. I would tell them that I'd meant to hug them and kiss them good-bye. Only then would I let the tears wash over my burning eyes.

But the days wore on and I heard nothing. Dark, fiery days that were silent as stone. No one came home. No one called out my name. Finally, I went to open the door. I could smell burning metal. I could see sparks in the trees, drifting like fireflies. All of those white pages on which I had planned to write my future were burning around the edges, first red, then black, then blue with flame.

My sister's dog refused to step past the threshold. He peed in a corner; he trembled and howled. Poor Onion was missing Aurora. His howls were like mourning cries. I couldn't listen to him, so I went outside and looked up at the black sky. My eyes were still burning, my vision was blurry, but even I could tell there were no stars. Ashes were falling down, a soft black rain. The white moths had dropped from above; they'd scattered like leaves, lining the stone path to our door, gleaming like black opals.

I found my way back to the top of the hill. There was only a handful of silver on the other side of the river now. Pale beacons, pale light. I thought about how time had always stretched out before me, those white empty pages that were mine alone. I thought about how hot it had been at the moment when it happened. How everything around me had been green as far as the eye could see. How the sky had been so cloudless, not even a puff of white.

As I walked back to my house in the dark, making my way past the brambles, I noticed that the songbirds who were usually asleep in their nests at this hour were fluttering nervously from tree to tree. It was then I realized it wasn't nighttime at all, but sooty daylight, noon perhaps. The sun had been shadowed by ashes. Now I understood. The world as I knew it was gone forever. What I had thought was the moon up above, as familiar as Aurora's face, was in fact the cloudy sun. On this day, even that circle of light looked so much smaller than it once had, a teardrop in the sky.

People in town must have assumed I had perished along with my family. No one came to search for me, and that was just as well. I was glad to be deep in the woods, away from them all. If anyone had tried to rescue me, I would have hidden behind our barn. I would have gone to the darkest part of the woods where the hedges were ten feet tall and the brambles cut the soles of your feet right through your shoes.

My grief was cold. It was nothing to share. It was nothing to speak about, nothing to feel.

I ate food from the pantry and kicked at the ashes in the garden. But I was lazy and did no work. What was the point? If this was the future, I wasn't certain I wanted to be in it. I started to feel as though I were disappearing. Perhaps I myself was a figment of my own imagination, a storm cloud, a wisp of smoke, a burning ember.

I could hear people singing in town; I could hear the church bells ringing. People were going about the business of living as best they could. They could see past today, into tomorrow. But not me. Grief had tied me in knots. There was no gas for the stove, but I didn't cut wood. There was no tap water, but I didn't go to the well. If I could have stopped breathing, I would have. I watched time moving, slowly, like dust motes, like gnats on a summer day, circling close, but never touching me.

I was so quiet and the house was so dark that anyone coming to call would have guessed there was no one at home. The looters who came must have assumed they had the freedom to do whatever they pleased. What I had was theirs for the taking. What I had was up for grabs.

As it turned out, I didn't hear a thing until they

were inside the gate. I was deeply asleep. I had fallen into sleep the way stones fall into a well. The looters had stumbled onto the property in the middle of the night and they didn't even pretend stealth. When I heard them shouting and screaming inside of my dreams, I awoke with a start, a cold band across my chest. The dog was whimpering, but thankfully he didn't bark. Silence was what we needed. Silence was all we had while they stole everything worth taking from the garden.

I crawled to the window and saw there were maybe a dozen boys and girls my age. They strode over the delicate seedlings with heavy boots, they pawed through the piles of ash I had planned to rake in their frantic search for anything to eat. They tossed lettuce and cucumbers and squash blossoms into the wheelbarrow they'd stolen from our barn. Whatever they didn't gorge on was loaded onto the wheelbarrow, till it nearly overflowed. Blackened peppers, singed peas, burnt cauliflower, all of it ripped from the garden. All of it gone before I could count to three.

I was quiet because I could tell they'd been drinking. There was the edge of something dark out there in the garden as they tugged and pulled at everything I had worked so hard to grow. Fights broke out. Words were slurred. I recognized a girl named Heather Jones I'd been at school with along with several boys from my classes. I thought perhaps they had also lost their families. I knew Heather's parents worked in the city. I knew they'd never let her run wild with a greedy horde such as this.

No one out in the garden looked like themselves in the black ashy night. The boys had painted their faces with mud and berry juice. The girls were all barefoot, in spite of the fact that there were still burning embers at the bottom of the piles of ashes. I had canned food in the pantry, maybe enough to share, but these intruders looked desperate. They wanted to take whatever they saw, they wanted to ruin anything that thwarted them, and the most I could do was crouch by the window and watch them. I was Green, who stayed in the shadows, who shivered and hushed the dog when it whimpered as the looters wrecked fences, tore out stakes, danced in the ashes. Green, who did nothing but shake while the troop in the yard destroyed everything in their path.

Perhaps they would have come into the house after that and taken whatever they wanted. Perhaps that was why one of the boys started up the path littered with fallen white moths. But a stone hit that boy square in the back, startling him. He stopped and turned to the woods. Something hooted out there. There was a cackle, human or animal — it was impossible to tell.

Afraid? several in the crowd called when he noticed the other boy had stopped on the path to our house.

More stones fell then, one after another. The cackle rose high, a hen, a ghost, a spirit, the wind. No one knew what it was, but the mob was not about to wait and find out.

Heather Jones ran away first, crying that there was even worse luck in store for those who stayed where they were. There should have been strength in numbers, but once the looters stopped wrecking things they were only boys and girls, easily frightened. The rest of the crowd soon followed Heather. Why shouldn't they go? They had already taken everything edible, piled into the wheelbarrow. They'd already had their fun.

When I went out in the morning, there was nothing left but ashes and stones. We had been at the height of our harvest, row after row of new zucchini and purple onions, of peppers that were shiny as frogs and blueberry bushes that were thickening with fruit. That garden was gone. Those days were over. Standing there, I knew my family wasn't coming back. I could feel it the way you can feel the wind across your face. Invisible, but certain. Sure as the blood in your veins.

I carried the stones, which had chased the looters from our garden, in all of my pockets. I took them far into the woods, out to where the oldest trees grew. Was it an accident that these stones had fallen, or was it something more? Should I be grateful to someone who had watched over me? I didn't know what to believe. I didn't know if I believed in anything at all.

Carefully, I made three piles: one for my mother, one for my father, one for my little sister. Every day I carted stones and every day I added to the growing stacks. Black for my mother, silver for my father, pure white for my sister, the hardest to find. The white stones tossed into our garden were best of all, they were like moonstones, aglow with light.

Wherever I went, I carried stones in my pockets, my hands, my boots. It was my duty, my burden, my gift, my soul, the reason I woke in the morning and went to sleep at night. Now I had a purpose, to build the stone stacks. I had known the woods before, now I knew them nearly blind and in the dark. I could find my way by touch. My fingers could tell the difference between east and west. I could rub a clod of dirt under my thumb and gauge how close to the river I was. Before long, I could hold a fallen feather in the palm of my hand

and tell whether it belonged to a jay or a sparrow or a dove.

When the stacks of stones were tall as the tallest men in the village, I went on to my next task. I began to clean the house. I was determined to get rid of all the ashes. I swept the floor until the straw bristles of the broom were ragged from use. I cleaned until my fingers hurt, and when it was done, when the brass doorknobs were shining and the kettles were scrubbed and the windows were bright with light, I turned on myself.

I chopped off all my burnt hair with the scissors my mother had used to trim the roses beside the front door. My hair was nothing more than a black curtain. I didn't need it anymore. My hair reminded me of my mother, it was the only way I was like her, the one feature we shared. I didn't want to be prideful anymore. I wanted to be as hard and brittle as the stones I carted into the woods, stones that could not feel or cry or see. That is what I wished for as I walked past the brambles, as I built the stacks in the woods higher and higher. I wished not to feel anything at all.

I had no idea that even in the darkest world, there are some wishes that can come true. Now I understand that those are the ones to think over most carefully. Those are the wishes that can wound just as surely as the sharpest arrow.

In no time, what I wished for, I became.

Soon enough, I began wearing my father's old black boots and a battered leather jacket that felt like armor. I kept several smooth rocks in my pockets along with a slingshot fashioned out of wood and a belt. I planned to be ready in case the looters came back. I smoked cigarettes I discovered in a drawer. I drank from the bottle of gin kept in the cupboard until my stomach burned. One night when the sky was ash-colored, I went into the ruined garden and clipped the thorns from the bare rosebushes, then sewed them to my clothes, one by one, until my fingers bled. Now I was ready to feel nothing. I was protected from feeling anything at all.

All the same, there was less and less food in the pantry and my stomach growled all the time. I hated it for wanting food. I didn't deserve anything, not food to ease my hunger or water to ease my thirst. I should have been on that street weighing vegetables when it happened. Instead, I had been weeding and thinking about my lunch. I was standing under the perfect, blue sky feeling sorry for myself.

That was when I took a pin and some black ink. I began to mark my arm. I outlined a raven, and then a bat, then a rose that looked like a flower found at the end of the world. That's who I was now without my mother and my father and my moonlit sister. Blood and ink. Darkness where before there had been patience, black where there'd once been green.

The decision of who would stay and who would go to the city was made arbitrarily that day, a single white page of fate that altered our future.

I could have insisted. I could have run after them. Then I would have been there to turn to my mother at the instant when it happened. The last thing I saw would have been her black hair and the fire behind her, red as roses.

But I was the one who was still alive, the girl whose eyes burned, whose vision was blurry, whose stomach growled, who wrote upon herself with black ink, as if that could change anything. Once, I had wanted only one thing: to be sixteen. One simple, easy desire. That day wasn't so far away, but it might as well have been forever. I was no more certain that my wish would be granted than I was that daylight would remain, that the birds would sing, that my garden would grow.

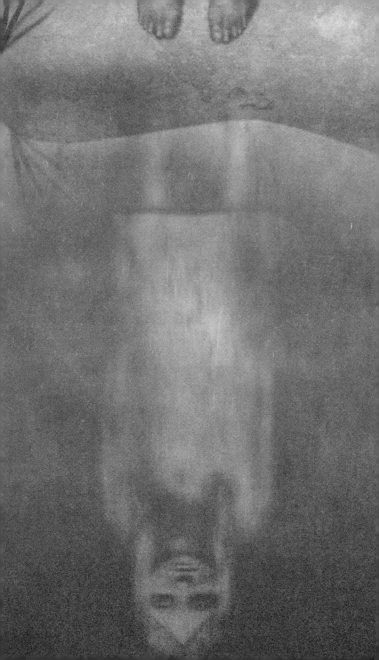

Soul

This is what I dreamed

Wanting only darkness, I began to sleep. I slept longer and longer. I ignored daylight and hope. I didn't care if the sky had begun to clear. Most of the ashes had fallen to the ground, leaving the horizon a faint washed-out blue. On several occasions I had noticed white clouds. There was the promise of sunshine. That wasn't what I wanted. I would rather sleep than eat or see the sky. Each time I put away my ink and pins, I closed all the windows. I drew the shades. When I went to sleep, under the table where I felt safer, I tied a scarf around my burning eyes so not even the tiniest bit of light could disturb me or remind me of what I had lost.

When I slept, I dreamed of the world as it was. My sister was clearing away the ashes. My sister was opening the window. Her hair was the color of moonlight, ice-colored, knotted from sleep.

Help me, she'd demand when the window stuck fast in my dreams, when the door wouldn't open, when the ashes were so deep she'd never be able to clear them away all alone.

I'd rise from my bed and do as she asked because I couldn't deny her anything. Once again, I was Green, who had patience. I was the girl with long, black hair who held the open book, white pages, empty and clean, black words flying like ravens, still waiting for the future, still hopeful, still me.

Whenever I dreamed and my sister was beside me, I could breathe easier. Aurora's skin was silver, aglow with light. Sometimes in my dreams she had grown up and was my age exactly. Even as my twin she was still my beloved opposite: the moon, not brackish green water. Bright, not dim. Wild, not plodding and shy. She was my sister and she knew my thoughts before they were spoken. She knew why I couldn't bear to see. Why I wanted the cinders in my eyes. Why I never bothered going to my mother's medicine cabinet, where there were so many ointments and cures. My vision was little more than shadows, but even in my dreams, I wouldn't search for a cure.

You know what you have to do in order to see, Aurora told me. She pinched me and pulled my hair to try to make me cry, but I wouldn't. Not in my sleep nor in my waking life.

My sister may have been cold as silver in my dreams, but she was as real to me as the candlesticks on the dining room table. As real as the moon climbing into the ink-black sky. As real as needles and pins. Each time I awoke, I felt her slip through my grasp, a cloud of mist evaporating in the light of day. If I couldn't see, if I shut out what was there before me and sleepwalked through my life, then I could go on dreaming. While I was sweeping the floor, while I collected buckets of water from the well, while I counted the jars of blackberry jam that were left in the pantry, first four, then two, then none at all, I was still with my sister.

Each night, before I slept, I took the black ink and tattooed ravens and roses and bats that could fly through the dark. Though I was almost blind, I could see well enough to do this. I could spy black ink, sorrow, loss, hearts breaking. I could see well enough to see that I was alone. I could see that soon enough I'd be starving if I didn't figure out what to do next.

I had picked all the blackberries that grew in the woods, all the blueberries, all the raspberries. I had found wild asparagus and made soups in the black pot I kept on the fire I left burning in the stove. My hands were rough from chopping wood, from gathering asparagus in the marshes, from collecting the few berries that hadn't been singed black from the heat across the river. There were very few tins left in the pantry, no flour, no salt. And my stomach went on growling, wanting me to stay alive.

I decided to go into town. But I wasn't a fool. I took precautions. I wore my leather jacket, my clothes with thorns, my heavy boots into which I had hammered half a dozen nails. I carried my stones and my slingshot. I was ready for looters, wild men, highway robbers. I expected almost anything, but when I left the woods for the main thorough-fare, all that greeted me was an unnatural silence.

There used to be traffic; there were trains that ran on the hour racing across the silver bridge into the city. Now the bridge had all but melted in the heat from the city. It was closed, a thick rope tied across the entrance. People stayed close to home, worried about what might await them on the open road. There used to be children headed to the river to swim on hot days; now there was no one. There used to be bicyclists, carts, farmers on their way into town to the monthly market; now there was nothing but the dust I kicked into the air with every step I took.

My sister's dog had followed me. He snarled at the few strays lurking about, pets left to fend for themselves when their owners failed to return home. On one corner there were two dead ravens, their feathers thick with ash. The plum trees that had lined the road were leafless, the bark gray. When I passed the church just outside the village, there was a sign printed with the names of everyone who'd been lost. One after another, mothers and fathers, sons and daughters. I was amazed by how many there were. But I was not surprised to see my name among them.

The girl I had been, the one called Green, they were right about her. She was gone.

The shopkeeper at the general store stared hard when he saw me. He didn't know who I was, with my short hair and my black ink and the nails in my shoes. He reached for the club he kept near his money box, ready to fight me off if need be. Even after I told him I was my parents' daughter, he didn't seem to believe me. He spoke to me from a distance, keeping the counter between us, as if he were conversing with a ghost.

Everyone said you were dead, he insisted.

I didn't dispute this. I didn't say these people were wrong. I just took what I'd brought to trade out of my backpack and held it up to the light.

The shopkeeper noticed my cloudy eyes; he could tell I was half-blind, and perhaps this was why he tried to cheat me. He told me the ring I had was copper. But I knew it was gold. My mother had kept this ring in a bowl on her dresser, and I had played with it ever since I was a baby. I knew what I held in my hands. Pure sunlight. Pure gold.

I laughed at the idea that my mother's most valued piece of jewelry was copper. The sound of my voice frightened the shopkeeper and he stepped even farther away. He didn't know what to expect from me, but one thing was certain. I wasn't shy anymore. I wasn't that quiet, moody girl Green, whom anyone could fool.

I was the girl who could touch the earth and gauge where to find the river. I was the one who could feel sorrow in the wind. I knew that gold was heavy, copper warm, and the silver candlesticks I brought forth from my backpack felt like ice.

I suppose you're going to tell me these are a deer's antlers, I said of the candlesticks, which had been cast by one of the finest silversmiths in the city. *I know what I have,* I told the shopkeeper. *I expect to be paid well.*

That was the last of any arguments at the general store. As a matter of fact, the shopkeeper called for his wife, who came to watch me with narrowed eyes, as if I were a circus act or a charlatan.

Green, the shopkeeper's wife said uncertainly. She'd known my family quite well and had often bought vegetables from my mother. But in the world we now lived in, why should she trust me any more than I trusted her? Why shouldn't she gawk at the nails in my boots, the slingshot in my pocket?

The shopkeeper and his wife tested my ability to distinguish by touch. If I could identify silver and gold, what else might I know? Sure enough I could tell green tea from black, navy beans from kidney beans, earth from ashes, honesty from deceit. I had another talent, it seemed. One that made people nervous.

After that, rumors flew around quickly enough. There were those who swore that anyone who touched my hand would be visited by bad fortune. I didn't disagree. I wanted the looters to hear about how I could turn the luck of anyone who came near me. And who was to say I wasn't cursed? I had lost my mother and my father and my sister, and sometimes when I caught a glimpse of myself in a shop window, I wondered if perhaps I hadn't lost myself as well. Every time I tried to say my name out loud the word stuck in my throat, a black stone, a silver stone, a stone as white as moonlight.

Before long, every shopkeeper on Main Street knew of my talents and my cloudy eyes. Even the looters, gathered under bridges and on street corners, were wary and stayed clear. In every store, people I'd known all my life hurried when I came to trade what I no longer desired for what I needed. They were forced to be honest with me, and they gave me what I'd come for. Gold and silver in exchange for cranberry juice, white rice, bandages, brown sugar, salt, vitamins. Coins and candlesticks for eggs, tins of baked beans, sugar, vinegar, laundry soap, candles.

There were good people in town who were helping out their neighbors and others who saw an opportunity for greed. Some people were busy cleaning the ashes out of the schoolhouse, while others were selling overpriced lanterns and oil and counting their profits. Honorable or not, most people were desperate for good fortune. Many hung horseshoes above their doors. They made certain to keep sprigs of rosemary nearby, to protect them from evil. But I knew better. I was defended with my nails and my thorns. I wore boots with nails, a scarf of black thorns.

One time when I was leaving town with my heavy backpack, a woman I recognized, a teacher of mine, called out for me to be careful on the road. She was kindhearted, and I remembered her lessons in language and history. But she wasn't my teacher anymore. I waved, but I hadn't learned anything new from her. I already knew that danger was everywhere.

I took a different route home each time to ensure that no one would follow Onion and me. I favored paths so rocky and steep, anyone else would have stumbled. It was the season when the earth turned red and yellow, when the whole countryside was blessed with orange light, but not anymore. Usually the leaves changed slowly: rubies, garnets, amber. This year, they had all dropped off at the same time.

This was the season when my sister and I had gathered fallen apples from the trees in our neighbor's orchard. The old woman would chase us away, shouting and throwing stones that dropped harmlessly on the grass. Now, the orchards were bare and the apple trees were as fruitless as fence posts. The hillsides were black; the road littered with garbage. Feral house cats living in the ditches would claw at any kindness, and Onion was so afraid of these wild cats, I had to carry him when they hissed and showed their claws.

I tried to avoid the looters who had wrecked my garden. I'd heard they'd taken up residence near the river, at a place made out of half-dead timbers they called the forgetting shack. Some slept beneath bridges, but they all gathered at the fire they kept burning when the dark began to fall. I could smell smoke coming from their direction. When I held up my hands to the east, where they were gathered, I could feel their pain, a kind of pain that was much worse than what I did to myself with my ink and my pins.

Once in a while, the looters arrived at a house in town in the middle of the night, threatening the citizens, demanding food. Most of them were no older than me, a few were only eleven or twelve. They had lost their parents, and, one by one, they'd run away from their empty homes. They drank gin until they were dizzy. They made themselves sick with whatever they found in their parents' medicine cabinets, tablets to make them woozy with dreams, pills that kept them up all night.

I had seen Heather Jones, the girl I knew who had joined them, panhandling on a corner. She had woven a hundred braids in her hair, and she wore what had once been a beautiful white dress. People walked by without looking, they didn't want to see the emptiness in her eyes, but I put some coins in her tin. I didn't wait for her to thank me. That's not why I did it. It was because I remembered the white dress she wore, how pretty she'd looked in school, how jealous I'd been. Now, the fabric was torn from the brambles she slept upon. Now, it was closer to gray.

I could hear the looters every once in a while, music rising from down at the forgetting shack at the river. I felt protected by my bad reputation and the nails I hammered into the trees all around my house, a warning not to come near. But sometimes I'd wake in the night and I'd listen to their music. I couldn't help myself. Voices carried on the wind, and their voices called to me. Several times, I'd left my sister in my dreams, and risen from my bed under the table. The loneliness I felt cut right through me, and not even sleep could ease my sorrow on nights such as these.

Help me, my sister called in my dreams, but I no longer went to her to help her carry water from the well, or sweep the floor, or close the window.

One night I went out very late. I made my way through the woods to see the forgetting shack for myself. I watched the looters dancing until their feet were bruised. Their bodies were covered with sweat. Some of them howled, and the sound went down my spine. Some of them spun in circles, until they looked like spires of silver.

Standing there alone, I swayed in time with the music. There were drums and tambourines. There was the organ they'd stolen from the church and the flutes they'd taken from the school music room. But this music was different from anything I'd heard before. It was something that scared me and made me want to be closer to it at the very same time.

I thought dancing with the looters would be like jumping into the fire. I would never have to think again. All I had to do was join them, do as they said, follow their lead, forget everything that had come before.

I laughed out loud at the notion and my laughter made them turn to me, all at once. The boys I'd gone to school with were all looking at me. Most of them had never noticed me before. Now I could probably have any one of them, if that's what I'd wanted. They were lonely the way I was. I could dance all night long with any boy I chose. I could forget right along with them.

They started to call to me as if they knew me. They started to come nearer. They thought I was Green, too shy to speak. Green, who had patience and pretty long hair. Green, who would dance with anyone who asked, anyone who grabbed her, anyone who pulled her closer to the fire.

Leave her alone, a girl shouted. It was Heather Jones in her dirty white dress. She was drunk, but she recognized me. *Does she look like she's one of us?*

Now the boys examined me closely. They saw the black roses and ravens on my skin. They noticed the nails on my boots, and my clothes, covered with thorns, so that anyone who tried to touch me would surely bleed.

They ran from me then, as though I were the dangerous one. They went back to their fire as if they'd never even noticed me standing so close by. I went home, grateful to Heather for calling out. She knew I wasn't like them. All the same, I understood what they were after. I understood wanting to forget. Things that made you remember cut like pieces of glass. A song, a memory, a blade of grass, a white dress, a dream, all of it as painful as the deepest wound.

I went home and locked my door. I was glad to be away from those pathetic creatures at the forgetting shack who didn't know how to face the darkness of their lives. That wasn't me. Heather Jones was right. I wasn't afraid of the dark. I didn't mind a certain kind of pain. I welcomed it because it took me away from my loss. It was better than anything at the forgetting shack. It was under my control.

I took the pins and the bottle of ink and held them close. Every night I tattooed more black thorns, vines, roses, bats. When I had less skin to cover, the task grew more difficult. I turned to my fingers and toes. My instep. My thigh. I had to squint and take my time. I worked hard, far into the night. Once I fell asleep still clutching my pins, spilled ink spreading across the table in a dark and endless pool.

Now when I dreamed, my sister took my hand in hers. She was still like moonlight, but fainter, more sorrowful. She whispered something I couldn't understand. It was as if we spoke different languages, as if I were losing her even in my dreams. The thorns on my skin were sharp and fierce, like me. The thorns could pierce through any dream. I grew restless in my sleep. I took to avoiding it whenever I could.

Green, my sister called to me whenever I grew so tired, I couldn't help but drift off.

It was the only word she spoke that I understood, but I couldn't answer to that name. Instead of tears there was soot in my eyes, so I called myself Ash. This was who I had become, but it was also the reason my sister stopped coming to me in my dreams after that. She didn't know me by name anymore, so how could she call to me?

When I closed my eyes to search for her, I was a stranger.

Treasure

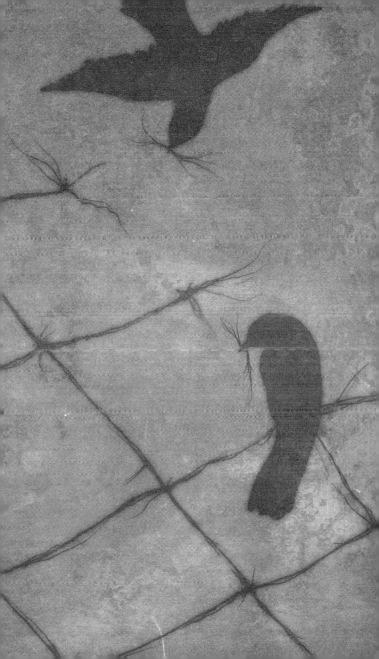

This is who I loved

I was gathering chestnuts deep in the woods where no one ever ventured, not even the crows, when I heard something nearby. Beside me, Onion began to growl, low in his throat, the way he used to whenever hawks came too close to our garden. Whenever there were strangers in the yard.

I bent to the ground, and I could feel footsteps.

At first I thought it might be the looters, come after me.

But when I touched the air, I could feel regret in the wind.

I thought it might be the girl, Heather Jones, with her neat braids and her ruined dress. Every once in a while she left her tin outside my gate. I filled it with bread or cooked rice or a bit of sugar. Sometimes I added a small pot of my asparagus soup.

But when I pushed away the overhanging branch of an oak tree in order to peer through, I could feel hope in the stems of the singed leaves.

The few birds that were left in the woods were chattering, flapping their wings, hopping from branch to branch. I could hardly see through the shadows, but when I narrowed my eyes I observed something white moving through the bare trees. It wasn't Heather in her torn dress. She slept most of the day, along with the others from the forgetting shack, exhausted from their wild nights.

I thought it might be a ghost that approached me. My sister, perhaps, with her snow-white hair, or my mother, in her favorite white shawl, or my father, his beard gone white with the shock of what had happened to our beautiful green world.

I dropped to my knees, not caring about sticks and stones. I could feel the thorns I had sewn onto my jacket and leggings stabbing through me. I wanted my family more than I ever thought I could want anything. Any bit of them, any piece would suffice.

If it were only a ghost that I'd found, that would have been enough for me. I wouldn't have asked for more. If it were nothing more than mist I could neither touch nor hold, formed into the shapes of those I loved, so be it. As long as I could see my sister, my mother, my father, I would pay any price. Accept any answer.

But it was no one I loved there before me. Not in spirit or in body. It wasn't a ghost or an angel or an enemy. It wasn't mist or cloud or memory. It was only a dog, a huge white greyhound. She was standing motionless, the scattered leaves on the ground turning to powder beneath her paws.

I grabbed Onion to make sure he wouldn't charge only to be snapped up by the larger dog in one bite. I carried my sister's terrier and the basket of chestnuts through the woods. I had traded away nearly everything that was worth trading, but I still had to eat. I had to quiet my churning stomach. Later, I would pound the chestnuts into flour and bake bread, but if I needed to defend myself against this strange dog on the way home, the chestnuts would work as well as stones when put to use with my slingshot.

Onion growled all the way home, so I knew the other dog was following. But I couldn't see her. I didn't hear a thing. She was a stray, like so many others, but something more as well. She was a ghostdog, mist through the woods, a pale cloud, silent and graceful. When I went inside the house, I could still feel her out in the yard. I put my hand on the cool glass of the windowpane, and there she was.

She felt exactly like sorrow.

That night I baked, and while the loaves of chestnut bread cooled on the rack, I went out to the porch. I alone sat on the steps where I used to sit with my sister, back when we thought the world was ours. If Aurora walked through the gate now, she wouldn't recognize me. She'd run from the ink on my skin; she'd shy from my choppy hair and the thorns that covered me, head to toe, front to back.

It seemed so long ago that we used to sit side by side, shoulders touching as we shelled peas for supper. Whenever we husked corn, we would toss the corn silk on each other's heads and laugh until we were dizzy. We were so certain of our futures back then. We were so sure of how we would fill up those blank, white pages. We would grow old together, marry brothers, live in houses so near to each other, we would be able to hear one another singing lullabies to the children we would surely have someday.

A few stars came out and shone, glittering and far away. The ashes had all fallen to the ground and I could see the moon, silver in the sky. Like a patch of moonlight, just as white, there was the dog in the garden. I waited, because I knew it would take time before she approached. I didn't blame her for keeping her distance.

After a while, my legs began to cramp up. I wanted to go inside and bolt the door. I wanted to sleep and close my burning eyes. But I stayed where I was, on the porch, in the moonlight. I dredged up whatever patience I'd once had, back when I was Green.

At last the white dog came closer. I didn't say anything. I was afraid I might scare her away. I knew what it felt like to be alone. I knew what it was not to trust anyone. All the same, I reached out my hand, the only part of me that wasn't covered with thorns. Now that the dog was beside me, I noticed that her paws were singed, the skin patchy and oozing and black. Greyhounds were meant to run, but every step must have brought this one agony.

When the greyhound rested her muzzle in my

outstretched hand, I understood why I'd thought she was sorrow. I would have never guessed that a dog could cry, but this one did. Maybe she'd been burned by embers, like the ones in my eyes, or maybe she'd lost everyone she'd ever cared about, the way I had.

I called her Ghost. When I said her name aloud she looked up at me, and when I went inside she followed the way ghosts do, silent, but there all the same. She curled up on the stone hearth, which was cool on her burned paws. Then she slept as though she hadn't had any rest for days, her feet racing through her dreams.

My own dreams were empty that night, devoid of moonlight. Even when I closed my eyes, my sister was always just out of reach. I started in my sleep and sat up, hitting my head. I was still sleeping in the pile of quilts under the dining room table. I'd been avoiding the room I'd shared with my sister; now I dragged along the pillows and quilt and went to open the bedroom door. There was moonlight streaming through the window, and before I knew it I'd fallen asleep in my sister's bed.

In the morning, it was as if Ghost had always been there. She ate from the same bowl as Onion, and the terrier didn't seem to mind. I found a salve in my mother's medicine cabinet, made from Saint-John's-wort and yarrow. I understood that a greyhound was not a greyhound unless it could run. I called the white dog to me, and she let me apply the ointment and wrap bandages around her paws.

That next night, Ghost slept at the foot of my sister's bed. I woke only once. I thought I had felt the dog running in her sleep. I thought I heard the sound of weeping, but when I stroked the greyhound's face, there were no tears.

The next time we went into the woods, I brought along a loaf of bread and a thermos of cold, clear well-water. I had planned to go back to where the old trees grew, to gather the last of the chestnuts, but Ghost had other ideas. She wouldn't follow. She led. Her paws were still so tender, she couldn't manage any more than a trot; still, I had to run to keep up with her. In no time my heart was pounding in my chest. How fast she must be when she ran at full speed. How much she must miss racing like mist. How sad that she was forced to plod through the woods with me as I stumbled through the brambles with my eyes that only saw half of what was there, with my nail-studded boots that slowed me down.

Before I realized where we were headed, we had arrived at my neighbor's house. The house was dark, and the front gate moved back and forth in the breeze. The yard was littered with debris, broken branches, black apples, clods of mud. Nothing grew in this place but nettles, tall and bitter, stinging to the touch.

This was the house that belonged to the neighbor who had thrown stones when Aurora took apples from her orchard. We had hooted and stuck out our tongues and made faces at her. We had run across her meadow laughing, but late at night we had wondered if she was a witch who might put a spell on us for eating the golden delicious apples we had gathered.

Now that I was beside my neighbor's door, I noticed a pile of the same white stones I had found in my yard, the ones that had been carefully aimed to chase away the looters, the ones that looked like moonstones. I hadn't given a moment's thought to this old woman, but she had obviously remembered me. I knocked on the door, and when no one answered, I pushed it open. I went into the house and there she was in her kitchen with nothing to eat but birdseed. Soot covered everything. The clocks no longer told time.

Have you come to return my stones? my neighbor asked.

I have something better to give you in return, I told her.

I left the bread and the thermos of water on the table, then I took the broom, the mop, the bucket, and began to clean. I was good at it by now. With one touch, I could tell what needed care. The books on the shelf were thick with dust. The floors were coated with muck. The paintings on the wall appeared black, until they were wiped clean to reveal women whose faces resembled my neighbor, younger, prettier relatives who looked down upon me kindly for rescuing them from the ashes.

When I had finished my work, everything in my neighbor's house gleamed. I had repaid my debt to her. Now I was the only thing covered in ashes. Ashes stuck to my skin, my choppy hair, the thorns on my clothes, my black tattoos.

Green, the old woman said to me. She had eaten every crumb of the bread I'd baked and drank every drop of water from my well. I wouldn't have guessed she knew me well enough to know my name, but it was too late to call me that now.

That's who I used to be, I told her. *Now my name is Ash.*

Whatever your name is, I have a gift for you in return. It's out on my porch.

There was only a big bag of birdseed, but I carried it with me. Once I'd reached home, I left the birdseed in the garden. I guessed it was worthless. I assumed it was all the old woman had.

My hands hurt from cleaning my neighbor's house. My feet ached in my father's old boots. My skin hurt from the sharpness of the pins. I had no time for worthless gifts.

Onion followed me into the house, but Ghost would not come inside for her dinner. I fell asleep in my sister's bed, exhausted. I woke once, and when I looked in the garden I saw the greyhound, white as the moon. She was tossing the bag of birdseed into the air as though it were a toy, shaking it with her teeth.

In the morning, there were a hundred birds in the garden. I sat on the porch where I used to sit with Aurora and listened as they sang a hundred different songs. The birds had converged from everywhere, from the deepest woods, from the charred canyons of the city. There were cardinals as red as cherries, jays as blue as the sky used to be, crows with night-black feathers, swallows with graceful wings, flocks of sparrows, mourning doves the color of tears.

When the hundred birds were finished eating,

the garden was littered with the husks of pumpkin and barley seeds. Something else had been left behind as well. Two baby sparrows, dusty and ash-covered, their wings too singed to fly. I took off my jacket and shook out the thorns, then carried the sparrows nestled in the jacket's lining. I brought them into the warm kitchen.

That night I dug until I found some juicy worms.

Is it all right to eat those? I heard someone say.

It was Heather Jones in her white dress, so skinny she looked like a ghost herself. She reeked of gin, and looked woozy. Her legs were covered with sores and little burns. Still, she smiled at me as though we had once been friends. I realized that Heather was prepared to eat worms. That's how famished she was.

I brought out some tins of beans, a loaf of bread, a few asparagus. I wished I'd had more. I'd been trying and failing to fish down at the river, and I couldn't think of anything else I could spare.

Then I remembered something I'd stored away.

I ran and found a dress that had belonged to my mother, soft blue denim that wouldn't be so easily torn by the brambles in the woods. Heather held the dress up to her carefully, as if it were made out of sapphires.

Oh, she said. *How beautiful.*

I thought about how jealous I'd been of her. She'd been one of the prettiest girls in school. By now we could hear music from the forgetting shack. We could smell the billows of smoke.

I'm late, Heather said.

You don't have to go if you don't want to.

It was as polite as I had ever been, and this was as good an invitation as I could manage, but Heather just laughed. She was unsteady on her feet. When you looked closely, you could see that her features were fine. So close to her, I could smell liquor and dirt.

Don't you hear? Heather insisted when I let her know she could stay. *They're waiting for me.*

Heather ran off with the blue dress, and there was nothing I could do about it. She thought they were waiting for her. She thought she could dance her sorrow away. She must have believed she could forget that her mother and father had also gone into the city that day.

I went inside to mash the worms into a paste. My hands were even uglier now from digging, from cleaning the old woman's floors, from chopping wood. I hardly recognized them as my own. I wondered if I was only a black cloud, a spray of mist, a stone, and nothing more. I studied the black roses ringed with thorns that I had inked onto my skin. I was Ash, and these were my hands.

But when I fed the worm paste to the baby sparrows they didn't care if my hands were ugly, that my burning eyes could hardly see, that my long, black hair was hacked off, lying in a pile in a corner. When I patted the dogs, they didn't care if my boots were old, if there was dirt under my nails, if there were thorns in my clothes, sharp as knives. When I swept my neighbor's floor, she had not cared that I was covered with ashes.

Every day I baked two loaves of bread, one to share with the dogs and the sparrows, one for my neighbor on the other side of the hill. My days were divided into tasks. I collected chestnuts in the morning, baked at noon, and late in the day I visited the piles of remembrance stones in the woods, white and black and silver. In the evenings, I took out my pins. I was covered now, my feet were covered with thorns, my legs with black vines, my arms with dozens of black roses. There were two ravens on my shoulders, and after propping up a mirror, I'd managed a bat at the nape of my neck. Every now and then I found room for a black leaf or an inky bud about to bloom.

As I worked, the sparrows nested in the pile of hair in the corner. A sparrow wasn't a sparrow unless it could rise into the sky, even I knew that. Soon enough the fledglings' singed feathers had fallen out, but I didn't guess how strong their wings had become until they began to flit around the house. I didn't know what they had been busy weaving in their nest until they presented me with their gift — a fishing net made from the strands of my own black hair.

I went down to the river that very night, as far away from the forgetting shack as I could. The moon was full. Streams of silver light reminded me of my sister. She would often dance while the rest of us worked in the garden. I used to tease her for being lazy. I used to call her names and tell her she'd never amount to anything if she didn't pay attention and work harder. Now I understood that she was working hard at dancing, at laughing, at being moonlight. She wasn't like poor Heather, forgetting with every step she took. My sister was learning the world as she danced. She was understanding the earth, the air, the fire of her own blood, the falling rain that made her laugh and dance even more wildly.

My vision was so bad, it didn't matter if I went fishing in the day or the night. In fact, my weak eyes preferred the moonlight. Night was better, colder, lonelier. But I was hardly alone. The dogs had followed me and the sparrows had fluttered behind, enjoying their first flight beyond the confines of the house.

Perhaps the fish would be more likely to drift into my net while they slept. I dipped my fingers into the cool water. I could feel the currents and the dreams of the fish, fluid and silver, like my own dreams had once been. I had tried to go fishing several times and had always failed at the task. But this time was different. It was the net that must have called the fish, dark and floating in the water, a broken part of me.

I caught three fish and placed them in a bucket of river water. I wrung out the black net and folded it into my pocket. The dogs followed me, the sparrows flew above me, the shining fish swam in the bucket I carried home. I cooked one fish for the dogs and the sparrows and me, another for my neighbor, and the third I kept in the bucket on my porch, where it swam in river water like a fallen star.

That night I dreamed of Aurora, but she didn't recognize me.

Where is my sister? she called out. *What have you done with her?*

Aurora still didn't know me by my new name. She backed away from the thorns and the nails and the black roses. I tried to run to her, but the vines around my legs pulled me down. I tried to reach out to her, but the thorns on my skin pinned me to the wall.

I heard someone crying, and when I awoke the cry was in my own mouth.

I went to the window to see if there were any stars. Out on the porch, something was studying the bucket where the last fish swam. It was a hawk that perched on the rim of the bucket, ash-covered, starving. The hawk hadn't been able to hunt because his beak had been burned. I wondered how long it had been since he'd eaten. We had always chased hawks from our gardens; we called them thieves and didn't like the way they scooped up the quiet rabbits and preyed upon the field mice who burrowed near the fences.

Now, I didn't drive the hawk away. I let him

make a dinner of the third fish, down to the eyes and the bones. I wished the hawk well, certain he'd soon be on his way.

But in the morning, the hawk was still on the porch, cleaning his feathers. I dressed and went outside. Without my leather jacket, I might have been afraid of his sharp talons, but I reached out my arm and the hawk hopped on. I treated his beak with lavender oil, which my mother always said could heal nearly any burn. I knew, after all, that a hawk is not a hawk unless he can hunt.

But for now he seemed happy to perch on my shoulder. So close to me, he felt like the wind, like the highest reaches of the sky. When we went into the woods to where the old trees grew, the hawk shook so many chestnuts from the trees, I could hardly carry them all home.

That day I had enough to bake six loaves of bread. One for me and the sparrows, one for the dogs, one for my neighbor, one for the hawk, one for Heather Jones, who had taken to sleeping under the old bridge where the weeds were as tall as trees.

I realized that there was one extra loaf of bread. I wondered why I had baked the sixth loaf, not knowing the reason until I heard footsteps out in my yard. They were quiet steps, not the looters, but the steps of someone who traveled alone.

I put on my leather jacket, my nail-rimmed boots, my thorn-edged leggings, then went to open the door. He was so very still I might have easily slammed the door shut without ever knowing he was there. I might have thought it was only the night outside, only the stars and the moon. But I could feel him out there, even though he was dressed all in black, his hood drawn low so he could hide in the ashes and no one could see his face. Just a profile. Just quiet.

Some other girl might have slammed the door and put the bolt on. She might have shouted for the stranger to go away or set the dogs on him. But I wasn't just any girl. I was the one with a talent for gauging truth from dishonesty, copper from gold, green tea from black, a friend from an enemy.

Though I could barely see his face, I knew this boy was a diamond. I could tell who he was when I touched his arm. I could tell from his boots coated with mud, from his black-hooded coat. I understood how alone he was and how tired he was of running. He seemed unable to speak, but the first thing he showed me was a small portrait of his mother that he'd painted. He carried the painting close to his heart.

The boy motioned that he'd been in the city, that he and his mother had been separated when the fire began. He had already crossed the river and walked a hundred miles to look for her. Now he was too exhausted to go on. His backpack was empty except for a box of paints and a sheaf of white paper, burned at the edges.

Another girl might have been afraid of a boy who arrived with so little, who refused to show his face, who could not speak a word. But I had my armor, I had my thorns, I'd already lost everyone

I'd ever loved. I offered the boy the sixth loaf of bread. I felt I had baked it for him even before he had walked into the yard. I could tell he was starving from the way he ate, huddled against the wind, his back to me. He wasn't about to let down his guard. He smelled like smoke and city streets.

I wasn't sure whether this boy had lost the ability to speak or whether he had simply chosen silence. Perhaps he spoke another language entirely. One I couldn't be expected to understand. That was fine with me. In silence there was truth.

I could tell who my guest was without one syllable. A boy who ran from the fire. A boy in search of his mother. When Ghost curled up at the boy's feet, when Onion didn't growl, when the sparrows ate crumbs from his hands, when the hawk perched on his shoulder, I knew I could let him stay.

I told him he could sleep in the barn. I brought out blankets and pillows. He could drink the water from the well. He could eat from the tins of food I had traded for in exchange for silver and gold and share the soup made from asparagus.

He could look at the stars with me whenever he liked.

When I told him my name was Ash, he nodded as though the word was a gift. Because he couldn't tell me his name in return, I called him Diamond. He seemed to like that name as well. Something inside him shone through the dark even though he kept his face hidden, hood pulled down. When he'd gone off across the yard to sleep, I thought perhaps I dreamed him up. A hallucination made out of loneliness, black ink, sorrow. Perhaps he'd never existed in the first place. But even when he'd gone and was already sleeping, I could see something bright everywhere he'd walked. It was almost like having moonlight again.

Rain

This is what I lost

Diamond didn't speak and I could hardly see; maybe that was why we got along so well. I, who preferred stones to flesh and blood, who kept away from people, could not spend enough time with Diamond. I knew him in a way I couldn't explain, the way I knew silver from gold, the way I knew the weather. When we listened to the wind together, we understood exactly what it was saying. When we sat close in the dark, we could feel each other's broken hearts beating.

Together, we stopped being hungry. We ate the bread I baked. Diamond fixed a soup out of beans and rice, simple but filling and tasty. Once, I asked him if his mother had taught him the recipe. Although he didn't speak, I could tell that the answer was yes. He took out the little painting of her, so carefully rendered in watercolors, and he didn't need to say more.

I knew he was thinking of her every time I heard him hum a certain tune, a lullaby she'd surely taught him. I hoped for his sake that his mother had managed to find safety when the fire began.

There was only one thing we didn't agree on. Diamond believed that the garden would grow. The topsoil was ashy and gray, and I told him not to bother with it, but Diamond wouldn't listen. All winter long, he carted the bad soil away. He spent hours picking out stones, which I brought to the piles in the darkest woods. Black for my mother, silver for my father, white as snow for my sister, a pile of moonstones.

You shouldn't even try, I told him each time he set to work. *Nothing will ever grow here.*

I showed him the looters' tracks, the broken fences, the pumpkin seeds left by the birds, the rock-hard earth. He just kept at it. I could hear him raking at night, as if he could work away his grief. For some reason I slept easier when I heard him. The sound of his working became as familiar as the wind, as rainfall, as the beat of a heart.

I still looked for Heather Jones. I worried that she would disappear, but it was easy enough to find her. During the daylight hours she was usually asleep under the bridge, her skin mottled from too much gin, the braids in her hair undone, her clothes dank from rainwater. I left pots of Diamond's stew for her, along with bottles of clean well-water. I knew Heather had been drinking from the ashy shallows of the river. She'd been eating mud just to fill her stomach.

Heather laughed sometimes when she recognized me, but it was the kind of laughter that sounded like a cry.

I could tell that she'd danced too close to the fire at the forgetting shack because she'd singed the hem of my mother's blue dress. She didn't seem to notice, and I didn't mention it. She was in a haze, trapped in the foggy ground between forgetting and living.

Still, we understood each other. If the world had been a different place, we might have been friends.

One day, Heather stared at me and grinned. She almost looked pretty. *Something's changed*, she declared. *You don't look the same.*

It was still me, my black tattoos, my leather jacket, my thorns, but Heather was right. I could feel a change inside, one I didn't yet comprehend.

When I went to my neighbor's to take her fresh water and fish I had caught with my net, I asked if she thought I seemed the same, the girl with ink on her skin.

The old woman didn't say a word. Instead, she led me to the staircase, where there were the ashy portraits I'd cleaned. Now my neighbor told me to try to guess which one she was. I studied the portraits carefully, but I had no idea which she might be. They looked familiar, but one girl was too pretty, one was too sad, one was too silly to be my neighbor.

Guess, my neighbor insisted. *Go on. Which one do you think I am?*

Still, I could not tell.

Look closely, she said, but even when I did, I had no idea.

At last I gave up. *Who are you?* I asked.

Each and every one, my neighbor told me. She shook her head as though I were a child rather than a girl about to turn sixteen. *Did you think nothing ever changed?*

Was it Diamond's arrival that had made the difference? Did it make it easier to listen to the wind with someone beside me? Wasn't the wind just as cold and harsh? Why would I feel any less abandoned? Wasn't I still alone in my thoughts? I already had the company of Onion and Ghost and the sparrows and the hawk and my neighbor on the other side of the hill. What did I need with this boy, who ate more than his fair share and filled the air with clouds of dust as he worked in the garden?

It was a puzzle I couldn't solve. After a while I stopped trying. Diamond was there, like the white dog and the sparrows and the hawk. A guest in my house, nothing more. He was there, like the wind and the stars up above.

I didn't understand for the longest time why I let Diamond stay. I watched him painting with the few watercolors he had left, and I felt as if something inside me was part of that paint, that white, singed paper, that paintbrush.

I didn't understand until one day when I went into the woods to search for chestnuts. That was when I realized I was singing. My voice sounded thin and unfamiliar to my own ears.

The next afternoon, I was wringing out the

wash to hang on the line when I realized I was dancing. My feet seemed too graceful to belong to me, even in my father's old boots.

The following evening, while I was polishing the last of the silver to trade, I happened to gaze into the platter my mother always used on holidays. Even I could see there was a smile on my face.

Something had indeed happened to me. This was not the way I ordinarily behaved. I was not someone who danced and sang and smiled at her own reflection. I was Ash, the girl with thorns on her clothes, the one who preferred stones to people.

When I next went to my neighbor's house I took along a pot of the stew Diamond had made. The old woman uncovered the pot and breathed in the scent of beans and rice. Then she told me to sit down.

She ladled out a bowlful for herself and one for me.

Did the boy cook this? she asked after she took one bite.

When I nodded, she looked at me closely, considering my face. The old woman had boiled a cup of tea for me, brewed from the stinging nettles that grew outside her door. I would have guessed the tea would be too bitter to drink, but the taste was perfect. It quenched my thirst completely.

You say your name is Ash, the old woman said thoughtfully.

I say it because it's true, I told her.

I had a tickle in the back of my throat. The feeling that some people get when they tell a lie. Quickly, I drank more nettle tea.

Is it?

My neighbor laughed then, as if she knew something I didn't know. She had already told me that everything changes. Now she wanted me to know more. She brought out a magnifying glass. When I peered through the glass I could see that one of the black vines tattooed around my ankle had turned green. It was the green of apple trees when they were first in leaf.

In my mouth, there was the taste of apples, sweet and sharp.

What do you think has happened? the old woman asked me. *Think hard.*

It's a trick of the ink, I told her. *Nothing more.*

All the same, I walked home slowly. I tried to figure out the puzzle I had become. I carefully tied the scarf of thorns around my neck. I kicked at the dust with my heavy, nail-studded boots. I didn't sing or dance or smile. I spat on the ground. I was Ash, after all.

But the taste of apples stayed with me.

In the evenings, after supper, Diamond sat at the table and painted. He hummed while he worked, and the sound made me think of what I had lost. I wished my sister could have danced to the song Diamond's mother had taught him. I wished when I closed my eyes, she was still with me.

I had no idea that Diamond was working on a portrait of me until he gave me the painting. At first I didn't know who it was. The girl I saw didn't look like me. There were no thorns, no nails, no bats, no vines, no black roses.

I'm not this pretty, I said. *My sister was the one who looked like moonlight.*

Diamond shook his head. He motioned for me to come close, and when I did, he touched my forehead.

I still couldn't see his face beneath the black hood. I couldn't see the look in his eyes. But I understood. I knew that he'd painted not only what he'd seen, but what he'd felt deep inside.

The next time I went to my neighbor's house I brought another pot of stew. On this day, the old woman had made bread out of nettles. Although this loaf was not half as sweet as the bread I baked, I ate every bit.

Do you still say your name is Ash? my neighbor asked when I had finished eating, when I had washed the plates and set them to dry, when I had swept the floor and straightened the portraits on the staircase.

It's still true, I told her.

She gave me the magnifying glass and told me to look at my hands. When I did I saw that the leaves that had been black were now green. It was the green of newly cut grass. In my nose, there was the scent of summer, fresh enough to make me sneeze.

I blew my nose on my handkerchief, but I could still smell cut grass.

It's the ink, I said. *Not me.*

I didn't believe the garden would grow, but I must have believed in Diamond. The next time I went into town I brought along my mother's pearl necklace to trade for packets of seeds. I had found the necklace in a drawer, set in a velvet box, tied up with ribbons. Beside the box was a card made out to me. My mother had planned to give me her pearls on my sixteenth birthday. Now I wasn't sure that day would come. The last thing I wanted was pearls. I thought my mother would understand and agree with me. I thought she would want me to choose lettuce and scallions and herbs above pearls.

I traded for the seeds and for something else — a denim jacket for Diamond. I thought it might suit him when he wanted to toss away that black coat with the hood that smelled like smoke. When he was ready to show me his face.

While I was getting ready to go I heard the shopkeeper and his wife talk about the people who had destroyed the city. Some of them had been living among us, pretending to be good neighbors. Their wives had shopped in our markets. Their children had gone to our schools, eaten our bread, played in our streets.

Many of their children had burned right along with others. Still others were wanderers, their families devastated. In the storekeeper's opinion it was easy enough to tell who these wanderers were. They would not look at you directly. Often they were burned. Even more often, they refused to speak.

I felt as though I had swallowed stones. Was it possible that my talent had failed me? That I had not been able to distinguish a friend from an enemy?

I walked through the woods without thinking of where I was going. I wanted to be lost, but I knew these woods too well. I could hear the music from the forgetting shack. I could hear laughter rising over the hill. I thought about the path that would lead me there. It was easy enough to find. I started down to the shack, slowed by my nail-studded boots. Halfway down the overgrown path I stopped. I had spied Heather.

She was curled up beside the fire, so close that sparks fell into her hair. People did their best to pull her away, but she crawled right back. She was long past listening to anyone. She was barely Heather Jones anymore. She was disappearing a little more each day, so thin, so frail, a wisp of smoke. One day she would surely vanish altogether, and there was no way to stop her. She was so busy forgetting, she couldn't take a single step into the future.

I turned and went through the woods. I wasn't interested in tablets or gin or sleeping pills or burning up alive. I had something far better to erase any facts that were too painful to remember. I could hear the hundred birds nesting in the tree-tops. I could hear the wind whispering that it would soon rain.

As soon as I got home I took out my blackest ink. I lit a candle, then sorted my needles and pins from the most delicate to the sharpest. I had one pin that was like a strand of silver, another that was like a sigh, a third that was as cold as a chip of ice, and a dozen more so tiny, I had to feel for them because they were all but invisible. Pain wasn't the thing I feared most.

I could hear the dogs running in their sleep. I could hear the sparrows fluttering their wings. Dreaming of the hunt, the hawk stretched out his great yellow talons. Diamond must have been asleep in the barn after a day of working in the hopeless garden. That was just as well. I didn't want to see him. I didn't want his silence, his black hood. I didn't want him as a friend or an enemy.

I could still see the bit of green on my ankle. That vine. That leaf. That rose. The color was a mistake. I wanted to announce who I was, not change back. I was Ash, who wanted black and stones, leather and thorns. I took my mother's mirror and rested it on a pile of my father's books. Now I could see my own handiwork, even with my blurry vision and the darkness of the night.

I had one place left, a circle above my heart.

I used the needle that felt like ice. It was the sharpest of all.

I was making a different sort of heart, one that was black, one that was protected by thorns, by bats, by raven's wings, by sorrow, by my aloneness, my armor.

I was halfway through this last tattoo when Diamond walked through the door. He was so silent, I could barely hear him. He was so quiet, I didn't know he was there until he took my hand in his. He raised the pin up to the place where his own heart was. He made it clear what he wanted me to do.

I gave him the other half of my heart. I worked until my fingers were numb, until our loss mirrored each other's. I used the ice needle, the one that caused the greatest pain.

I watched to see if Diamond flinched, but he never once did. I etched half a rose, half a wing, half a thorn, half a leaf. When I was done, Diamond took off his black hood so I could see what the fire had done to him. Then I understood why pain meant nothing to him anymore. I could see why half was enough for him. One side of his face was perfect, my Diamond. The other half was charred and discolored. I kissed both sides. They were one and the same to me.

I could feel the season changing. It was growing warmer every day. I felt it as though I were a leaf that was greening, a vine that was growing toward the sun.

One day the sparrows rose high in the sky, then

settled in the treetops. I forced myself not to call them back to me. I knew they were meant to fly.

Soon after the hawk disappeared from my porch. I would see him sometimes, his wingspan nearly blocking out the sun. He peered down from above, but I didn't whistle for him. I didn't wave so that he would light on my arm. I didn't insist that he eat grain from my hand. I knew that hawks had to hunt.

All the same, I considered putting a collar and a leash on Ghost. I knew she was next. I could tell by the way she stared into the woods. One morning when the air was especially fresh and Diamond was watering the garden, I left Onion inside the new fence Diamond had built. I felt the leaves, the vines, the warming air. I went out walking with Ghost.

We went past the oldest trees, past the piles of stones, to the deepest part of the woods. Even I who knew these woods so well could have lost my way here, but the white dog knew where to go. We both knew what she needed to do.

In the treetops there were the hundred birds who had come to eat birdseed from my garden. There were the sparrows who had knitted a fishing net from my own black hair. There was the hawk whose wingspan could block out the sun.

I knelt down beside the white dog. I could feel her trembling. That's how badly she wanted to run.

She had slept on my sister's bed with me. She had dreamed right alongside me. She had led me to places I never would have gone if I hadn't followed her. She looked up at me, and I called her Ghost one last time. Then I let her go.

Not long after that, Heather Jones disappeared. She was not at the place where she usually slept, beneath the bridge. When I left out food and clothes for her, no one collected the packages. When I looked for her footsteps in the mud, they weren't there.

I went down to the forgetting shack to search for her. It was early morning, and most of the people there were still asleep. Their feet were bloody from dancing all night. Their hair was threaded with brambles. I found two girls I might have recognized if they hadn't been so filthy and so drunk. They were settling down to sleep, but they nodded when I asked about Heather. She was gone, it was true. No one had seen her for days.

There were those who wondered what had happened to her, but they were too tired to look for her, too busy forgetting. Some people said she had drifted into the fire as she danced one dark night. She had tripped, she had fallen, she had turned into smoke. When I looked in the fire they always kept burning, there were bits of blue among the ashes.

When I left the forgetting shack, I went to visit my neighbor. My nail-studded boots hurt my feet, my leather jacket slowed me down, but at last I reached the old woman's house. I thought about Heather Jones. I thought about how it was impossible to forget, no matter how hard anyone might try.

I knocked on the door, and the old woman was waiting for me. She had made a soup out of well-water and nettles. It was thin and lukewarm, but the taste was just what I needed, bitter on my tongue.

Tell me your name, my neighbor said.

I could see the girl my neighbor had once been reflected in her eyes, in the way she held her hands, in the way she laughed at me now.

Speak up, she said. *Say it out loud.*

Ash, I insisted. *Only Ash.*

My neighbor handed me the magnifying glass, and when I looked at my arms I could see that each black rose I had inked there had turned white with a green center, the night-blooming flowers of my dreams. I could feel something green growing inside me. Green as summer in my bones. I ran all the way home. I ran through mud and brambles and thorns.

But I could feel it still.

If sparrows were meant to fly, and hawks to hunt, and greyhounds to run, then a boy such as

Diamond was meant to search for his mother. If he didn't go, if he forgot or thought of himself first, then he wouldn't be Diamond. I knew that. I wasn't surprised when I reached the gate and saw him standing there, carrying his backpack, wearing the denim jacket I'd gotten in exchange for pearls. I understood why he couldn't stay.

So I gave him a map, a thermos of clear water, a loaf of the bread I had baked. I gave him half of my heart to take with him, no matter what road he turned onto.

If he'd had a voice he would have said good-bye, he would have told me he would surely miss me the same way I'd miss him. Instead, he held me close before he set out toward the road. Instead, he kissed me and I knew these things without a single word being said.

Sister

This is the story I tell

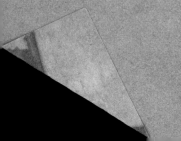

My sister came back to me in my dreams. I could see that Aurora wasn't my age. She wasn't my twin. She was only a little girl, one I would miss every day of my life. Now that I was Green again, Aurora recognized me. She called out my name, and I was Green through and through.

I told my sister I didn't think I could live without her, but she assured me that was something I would never have to do.

I'm with you forever, she told me.

Right away, I knew it was true. True for my father, who could whistle to the birds in the trees. True for my mother, who had such gentle hands. True for my sister, who shone like silver.

When I woke from my dream I was crying. I cried like the rain, like the river that flowed to the city, and all my tears were green. At last my eyes were cleared of embers. At last I could fully see. There was daylight out my window. There were the seedlings Diamond had grown in the garden. There was the world waiting outside, aching and ruined, but beautiful all the same.

I went out and worked until I was sweating in the sun. While I worked, I missed my father and my mother. I missed the white dog and the sparrows and hawk. I missed Diamond and I missed Heather Jones.

Most of all I missed my sister.

I thought about them every day. I thought about them while I weeded between the rows, ked the ground with well-water, while I hat was left of the ashes. Before long, the vines from the pumpkin seeds left by the sparrows were a hundred yards long. The seedlings were as high as my waist. By spring, the vines of sweet peas were taller than I was. When the warm weather returned, Onion could hide between the stalks of corn. There were hundreds of blue jays and sparrows that came to sing to me while I worked. There were white clouds drifting across the sky.

It was so hot, I took off my leather jacket. I took off my scarf made of thorns, my father's old boots. At night I dreamed of my sister, and she knew me as well as I knew myself. I dreamed of vines and grass, apples and emeralds, rain and white night-flowers that bloomed with green centers. I dreamed of everything I'd lost and all that I'd found and everything in between.

On the day I turned sixteen, I went to stand on the hillside. There were more and more lights to be seen on the other side of the river. People were moving back. The city was being rebuilt. Go¹ by daylight, silver at night. I could hear hammering as people from our town rebuilt the bridge. They worked all hours, they used every nail in the county, every spare set of hands.

By the end of the growing season, I'd be able to take my vegetables into the city. I'd buy myself a scale and measure out the peas and the peppers carefully, as my mother always had. I'd whistle the tunes my father had loved. I'd shop at the stores that had been both my sister's and my favorites: the bookstalls, the candy kiosks.

Wherever I went, gold dust would stick to my feet. Silver would shine in my dark hair. On every avenue, every street corner, every sidewalk, I'd carry my sister close to me, inside my heart.

Today, on the first day of being sixteen, I took three stones and went far into the woods. Without the nail-studded boots, I no longer tripped over brambles. Without the leather jacket, I did not tire. Wi.... he scarf of thorns, I could move .... s like mist.

When I reached the three stacks, I bowed my head. I listened to the birds, a hundred different songs of sorrow and forgiveness. That morning the first thing I'd done after waking was to go out and search until I'd found one perfect black stone, one perfect silver stone, one stone that shone white as the moon. They were the last stones I would bring here. I knew they were the last because they felt light in my pockets, light in my hands. I knew because I could remember without them.

When I left the woods to celebrate my birthday at my neighbor's house, it was twilight. All along the hillsides, everything looked green in the fading light. A few of the oak trees had managed to send out some wavering leaves. The hardiest plants, witch hazel and old ferns, were growing in the ditches. I took my time and watched the green in all its shades. I treaded gracefully, as my mother once had. I took even strides, as my father had. Onion followed me, as he used to follow my sister.

When I arrived at my neighbor's house she

went to the stove and ladled out a stew made from all the vegetables I'd brought her. It was a gift from Diamond, every bit of it. It was the garden he'd grown when I'd still refused to believe in anything. Sometimes I wondered if he hadn't watered the seedlings with his tears, and if the tears hadn't turned to silver. Everything he'd grown was filled with light.

When we'd devoured every spoonful of our dinner, my neighbor brought out a cake made of nettles. There was no icing, no candles, and the color was faintly green. A cake such as this should have been too bitter to eat, but I found I preferred it to any I'd had before. I ate every crumb, and still wanted more.

What do you call yourself now? the old woman wanted to know.

She didn't have to ask twice. For the first time since the day when it happened, I said my name out loud. The word tasted sweet as apples, fresh as grass, fragrant as roses. When I looked down I could see that the half-tattoo I shared with

Diamond had turned green around the edges. In the center, it was red.

My heart was opening.

You made it happen, my neighbor told me. *You are the ink,* she said. *Write as you want.*

It was Green who thanked the old woman, who ran home, greener with every step. Green, who was covered with bright vines, with roses that had emerald centers and only bloomed at night. Green, who threw away the ragged scarf, who cast off the leather jacket, the old boots, the ravens, the bats, the thousand thorns.

I went to the table and opened the bottle of ink, meaning to spill it all out. By chance, I took a pen and dipped it in the bottle. I saw then that the ink was green. It was the ink of a sister, a woman with long, dark hair, a man who was strong. It was the ink of a witness, of a girl of sixteen who had no idea what the future might bring. Green as the world we once knew.

I found a ream of white paper in a desk drawer. Then I understood the path my mother had spoken of for me. Every white page looked like a garden, in which anything might grow.

I sat down at the table with the pen and the ink. I spread out the clean, white pages.

Then and there, I began to tell their story.

With gratitude and love

to my dear publisher, Jean Feiwel,

and my wonderful editor, Elizabeth Szabla.

Many thanks also to Elizabeth Parisi

for her brilliant design.

To Matt Mahurin, thank you, thank you,

for pure genius.

About the Author

ALICE HOFFMAN is the author of numerous
acclaimed and best-selling novels which have
been published in more than twenty languages, including *Illumination Night*; *At Risk*;
Seventh Heaven; *Turtle Moon*; *Practical Magic*, which
was released as a major motion picture; *Here
on Earth*, which was an Oprah's Book Club
selection; *Local Girls*; *The River King*; *Blue Diary*;
and *The Probable Future*. Her novels for
Scholastic include the acclaimed *Aquamarine*
and *Indigo*, paired in the volume *Water Tales*.
She lives with her family outside of Boston.

Visit Alice Hoffman at www.alicehoffman.com.

Further enchantment from Alice Hoffman

ALICE HOFFMAN'S
Water Tales

TWO NOVELS

Aquamarine & Indigo

From the best-selling author of *Green Angel,* two magical tales that sparkle like drops of water after a storm. In *Aquamarine,* a mermaid comes ashore seeking true love. In *Indigo,* two unusual brothers long for oceans they have never seen. Magical and mysterious, these are tales to fall in love with.

$5.99/$8.99 CAN

Available in paperback wherever you buy books.